The night before the team went to Bobblesberg, Scoop had a nightmare. He dreamt he was on television, taking part in a skiing competition.

"And here comes Team Leader Scoop. The fastest digger on the slopes!" said the commentator. "He's off to a flying start... oh dear! That didn't look good! He's gone off piste!"

Scoop flew through the air, out of control.

"Ahhh! Bob, watch out!" Scoop shouted, as he smashed through the log shed Bob had just built and landed head first in the snow.

"Oh, no! It's all over for Scoop! He's snowed under!" shouted the commentator.

Next morning, Scoop told Pilchard all about his nightmare. "I'm worried about the big job we've got in Bobblesberg at the Winter Games," he explained. "Bob has asked me to be team leader. But what if my nightmare comes true and I really let Bob down?"

Pilchard didn't think Scoop would let anyone down.

"Oh, goodness! Look at the time. We've got a ferry to catch!" sighed Scoop. "Bob! Bob! Wake up!"

Bob appeared at his window in his pyjamas.

"Oh, sorry team! My alarm didn't go off," Bob yawned. "Luckily I can rely on you, Scoop."

Farmer Pickles was going to look after Pilchard while Bob was away. Spud and Travis arrived to collect her.

"Goodbye, Pilchard," said Bob. "Be a good girl."

As the team left to catch the ferry, Pilchard jumped down from Travis's trailer and hid in Scoop's back digger. When Spud and Travis realised that Pilchard was missing, they rushed to the ferry port to see if she had gone with the team. They arrived just in time to see her poking her head out of Scoop's digger as he and the team boarded the ferry.

"Oww! Come back Pilchard!" Spud shouted. He jumped aboard the ferry.

"Wait here for me, Travis. I'll catch her before the ferry leaves," cried Spud, as he chased after Pilchard.

As Spud caught up with Pilchard, the ferry blew its horn and steamed out of the harbour.

"Owww, no! We're on our way to Bobblesberg," sighed Spud, as he looked over the rails and out to sea.

Meanwhile, Bob was talking to the team.

"In a few day's time, Bobblesberg is having a Winter Games competition with our town, Bobsville. We're going to build a log cabin for Bobsville's Mayoress to stay in," explained Bob. "I want this job to be the best one we have ever done. **Can we fix it?**"

"**Yes, we can!**" shouted the team.

When the ferry arrived later that day, Bob and the team had to travel through the mountains to get to Bobblesberg.

"Phew! I thought that tunnel would never end!" sighed Bob as they came out of a very long mountain pass tunnel. "Oh wow!" he gasped as he saw the view.

Bobblesberg town sat at the foot of the mountains below.

"It's amazing! That's the most beautiful town I have ever seen!" sighed Scoop.

"Oh, yes!" cried the rest of the team.

As they entered the town, they heard a band playing wonderful music and someone singing at the top of her voice.

"Yodl-oh-ooh-hee-hee!" sang the singer.

"Ha, ha, ha!" giggled Dizzy. "That's funny singing!"

"It's yodelling," explained Roley. "It's very hard to do, actually."

"Hi, everyone," greeted Wendy, when she spotted Bob and the team listening to the band. "Did you have a good journey?"

"Yes, thanks Wendy. We even had a couple of stowaways!" laughed Bob, pointing at Spud and Pilchard. "So I see!" chuckled Wendy. "Come with me everyone. I'd like you to meet someone."

"This is Jana von Strudel and her goat, Eli," announced Wendy. "She's in charge of the Winter Games, and she's a pretty good yodeller, too!"

"Well, I try! Yodel-odel-odel-ee!" sang Jana.

Then Jana introduced Bob to a ski-doo. "This is Zoomer. He will drive you around while you are here."

Wendy took Bob and the team to their hotel. Spud and Pilchard had nowhere to sleep so Charlene, the hotel manager, said they could share Bob's room.

"Wow! A scarecrow could get very used to this!" grinned Spud when he saw the room.

"No worries mate! Call room service if you need anything," said Charlene.

Zoomer checked that the machines were comfortable in their shelter, outside the hotel. "There'll be more machines here tomorrow," said Zoomer.

"What machines?" asked Scoop anxiously.

"Special machines for building the courses for the games," Zoomer explained. "They're amazing!"

"Oh, I see," said Scoop. "Now get a good night's sleep," he told the other machines. "We've got a busy day tomorrow."

But next morning, Jana brought
bad news. A snowstorm had blocked
the road to Bobblesberg, and the special machines
could not get through. The Winter Games would have
to be cancelled.

"Why don't **we** build the courses?" Scoop suggested.
"Bob always says we can do anything."

Just then, one of the special machines appeared. He'd
arrived before the snowstorm started.

"I'm Benny," he announced. "I build ski runs and ski jumps."

"We could work with Benny," said Scoop. "He could show
us what to do."

"That's a very good idea," Jana told him.

The next morning, Spud offered to help Charlene serve breakfast as she was very busy.

"Spud's on the job!" he giggled as he handed Bob and Wendy their breakfast.

As they were eating, Scoop called to them through the hotel window.

"Jana nearly cancelled the games because the special machines can't come and build the courses," he gabbled. "So I said we would do it, and Jana thinks it's a very good idea."

"But we've never built courses," Bob argued.

"Benny can help. He's a specialist machine. He and I can build the courses while you build the log cabin."

"That's a good idea," said Wendy.

"OK, Scoop," Bob agreed.

Benny showed Scoop how to build a ski run with moguls.

"They're the lumpy, bumpy bits," he explained. "Next, we'll build a couple of ramps and some control gates."

Meanwhile, Bob and the rest of the team were building foundations for the log cabin. When they'd finished, Bob went to see the ski run.

"Benny showed me how to make the moguls and I did all the work myself," Scoop boasted.

"I'm very proud of you," Bob told him. "I only need Lofty now to build the log cabin so I'll send Muck, Dizzy and Roley over to help you."

When they arrived, Benny and Scoop were throwing snow onto the ground to make a ramp. Muck thought it was a game, and hurled snow at Scoop. Everyone laughed.

"It's not funny," spluttered Scoop.

Then Roley flattened some moguls by mistake.

"You big clumsy lump," Scoop shouted angrily.

The other machines stared at Scoop in horror. He was being so bossy and unfair.

While Scoop repaired the moguls, the others helped Benny build the ramps. But they practised yodelling like Jana while they worked, and that made Scoop even crosser.

"I can't work when you are being noisy," he complained. "Go and find something else to do."

"Hmm," said Bob, when Muck told him about Scoop. "He will need your help with the Bobsleigh run, which is his next job. I'll go and check on him."

Muck had nothing to do so he suggested to Zoomer that they had a race. But as they set off, Muck drove onto a wooden panel. The panel began to slip down the mountain...

"Wahay," yelled Muck happily. "This is fantastic, I feel like I am flying!"

"Is this what they call snowboarding?" asked Lofty.

"Being team leader has changed Scoop," said Dizzy, as she and Roley trundled across the snow.

"I don't think he means to be grumpy," said Roley. "He's just worried."

Two children were skating on a nearby frozen pond.

"Hey!" cried Dizzy. "That looks brilliant fun."

She hurried onto the ice and spun round and round.

"I'm whizzy Dizzy," she squealed. "Come and try this, Roley."

But Roley could hear Jana yodelling up the mountain.

"I'm going to find Jana," he told Dizzy. "I want to learn how to yodel properly."

On his way up the mountain, Roley met Jana and Eli, her yodelling goat.

"Can you teach me to yodel, Jana?" Roley asked.

Jana said she would. She explained how people used to yodel messages to each other across the mountains.

"Copy me," she instructed.
"Yodel-odel-odel-aye-ooh-ah!"
"Yodel-odel-odel-aye-ooh-ah!"
sang Roley.
"Very good-el-odel-odel-ee!" Jana sang back.
Then she sent Roley and Eli up another mountain, and they
yodelled to each other across the valley.

Down at the log cabin, Bob and Lofty were admiring the finished roof.

"I'll go and check up on Scoop," Bob said, and zipped off across the snow on Zoomer. On the way he saw Muck snowboarding.

"Come with me," Bob told him.

Scoop and Benny were struggling to dig the Bobsleigh run.

"Oh dear," said Bob. "You'd better get stuck in, Muck. Scoop will be here for a week otherwise, and he still has the ski jump to build today."

"Muck to the rescue," laughed Muck.

Scoop didn't like that at all.

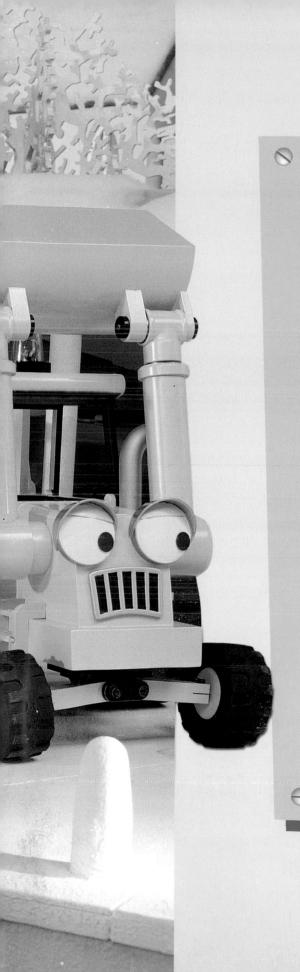

That night in the shelter, the machines were chatting about their day.

"Quiet, I'm trying to sleep," Scoop complained. "We're here to work, not to have fun."

"But you won't let us do any work," Roley pointed out.

"Remember what you did to the moguls?" asked Scoop.

"Everyone makes mistakes," said Muck. "Even you."

"We're all good at different things," Dizzy explained. "That's why we're a team. You're no better than us."

Scoop stormed out of the shelter.

"Tomorrow I'll build the ice rink all by myself," he muttered. "That'll show them."

When Pilchard saw Scoop sneak off early next morning, she woke up the machines. But only Benny went to help Scoop.

"To build the ice rink properly you'll need the team," Benny explained.

"And you need to stop telling me what to do!" Scoop retorted.

"Fine, do it all yourself!" yelled Benny, and drove off.

When Scoop had built the ice rink, he towed a machine onto the ice to smooth it. But Scoop couldn't control the machine and suddenly, there was a terrible cracking sound. The ice broke up into lots of pieces and the barriers fell down. The ice rink was ruined!

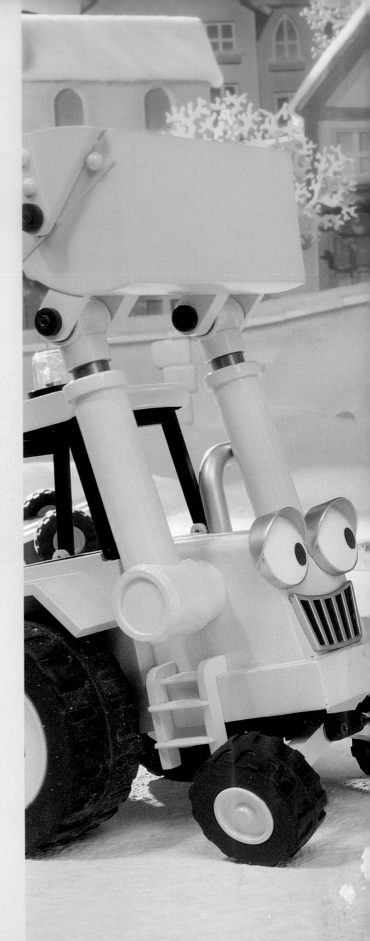

"I don't know what to do," Scoop cried. "The only way I can get this job done is with the team's help, but I've been horrible to them, and I don't even know where they are to say sorry."

Pilchard took Scoop to find the machines, and they all accepted his apology.

"Please can you help me fix the ice rink?" begged Scoop.

"Yes, we can!" they replied.

"Thank you, Pilchard," Scoop whispered to his friend.

And working together the team fixed the ice rink.

After her morning ski, Jana joined Bob and Scoop at the ice rink. Bob was admiring the work.

"You've done a great job, Scoop," said Bob. "I'm very proud of you and the team."

"Yes, your machines are very special," agreed Jana.

"Thank you," said Bob. "Now, let's have some fun before the games start!"

The day of the **Winter Games** was a great day for Bobsville. Wendy broke the Bobsville skiing record. Bob and the team were very proud of her. Everyone had fun playing in the snow. And Eli, Spud and Pilchard enjoyed riding on the ski lift!

Then at the end of the games, Spud, who had been helping Charlene sell drinks and snacks, slid down the ski jump holding a tray full of drinks, spun through the air and landed without spilling a drop!

"**Spud's on the job!**" Spud roared as he flew through the air.

"I bet you didn't expect to see Spud on your ski jump, Scoop," Bob laughed, as he watched Spud land.

But Scoop was fast asleep…

Scoop dreamt they were at the Dream Machine Team Games. Bob and Wendy gave each machine a medal, and then Jana and Eli yodelled their team song.

"So, Scoop," asked the television commentator, "How are you feeling?"

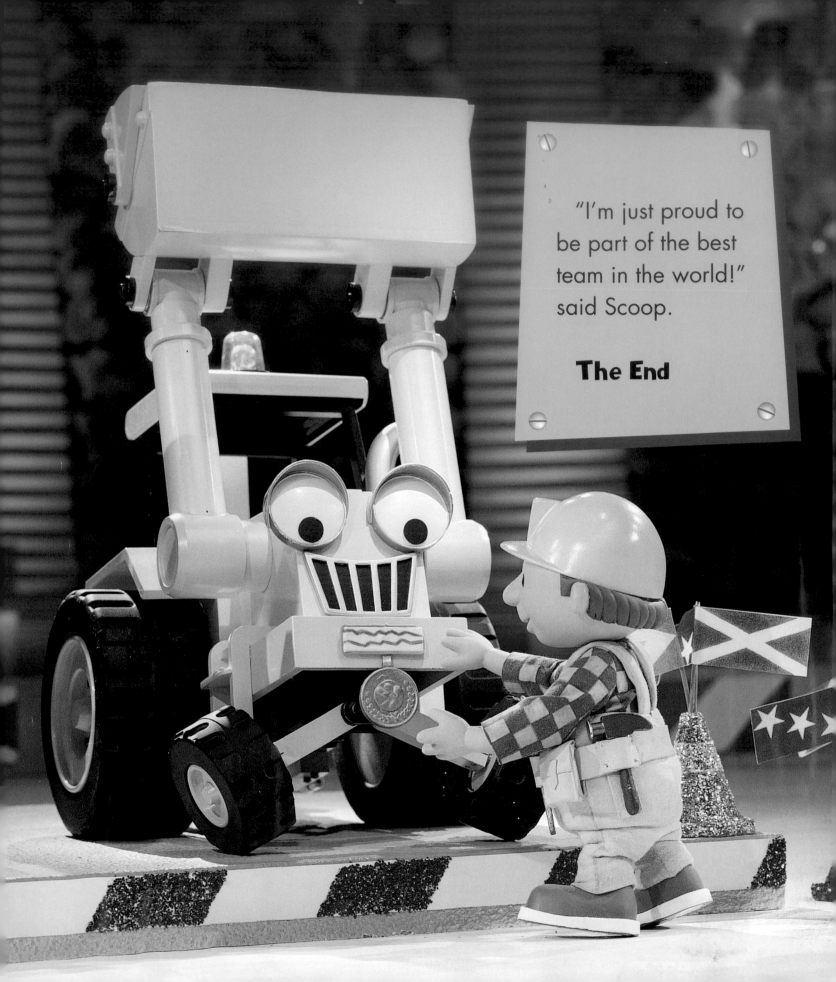

"I'm just proud to be part of the best team in the world!" said Scoop.

The End